# Dazzling Dribbling!

## Michael Coleman

### Illustrated by Nick Abadzis

ORCHARD BOOKS

With many thanks to
Mark Kinder and Leon Pyrzewski of
Fareham Sacred Heart FC, for telling me what
it's like to play football wearing glasses – and
how difficult it is trying to play without them!
M.C.

ORCHARD BOOKS
96 Leonard Street, London EC2A 4RH
*Orchard Books Australia*
14 Mars Road, Lane Cove, NSW 2066
First published in Great Britain in 1999
First paperback edition 1999
Text © Michael Coleman, 1999
Illustrations © Nick Abadzis, 1999
Cover photograph © Action Plus
The rights of Michael Coleman to be identified as the author
and Nick Abadzis as the illustrator of this work
have been asserted by them in accordance with the
Copyright, Designs and Patents Act, 1988.
A CIP catalogue record for this book is available
from the British Library.
1 86039 742 5 (hardback)
1 86039 950 9 (paperback)
1 3 5 7 9 10 8 6 4 2 (hardback)
1 3 5 7 9 10 8 6 4 2 (paperback)
Printed in Great Britain

# Contents

Coach

Midfield
(Centre)

Left Full
Back

Striker

Right Full
Back

Centre
Back

Goalkeeper

Kirsten
Browne

Barry 'Bazza'
Watts

Daisy
Higgins

Colin 'Colly'
Flower

Tarlock
Bhasin

Lennie
Gould
(captain)

Trev the
Rev

Substitute

Midfield
(Centre)

Centre
Back

Substitute

Midfield
(Right)

Striker

Midfield
(Left)

Mick
Ryall

Jonjo
Rix

Lulu
Squibb

Jeremy
Emery

Rhoda
O'Neill

Lionel
Murgatroyd

Ricky
King

# 1

*Mick Sees a Problem!*

"How about these for next season, everybody?" said Trev brightly, dipping into the holdall at his feet. "I've been given them for nothing! What do you think?"

The Angels coach held the orange football shirt aloft. Seated in a semi-circle around him, the Angels players gaped silently up at it, then at each other, then back at the shirt again.

It was Lennie Gould, the Angels captain, who finally broke the silence.

"Given 'em for nothing, do you say? Then you woz robbed, Trev!"

"Very witty, Lennie," laughed Trev. "Seriously, though. What do you really think of it?"

Mick Ryall, the team's tricky right midfield player, took off his glasses, blinked, put them back on again and said, "It's bright, Trev. It's definitely bright."

"Bright!" cried a shocked Bazza Watts. "It's near enough luminous, Mick! I've seen car headlamps that don't glow as much as that shirt!"

"Going to be playing night-time matches next season are we, Trev?" asked Lulu Squibb sarcastically. "Y'know, without any floodlights?"

7

"I thought you might like to try them out tomorrow," said Trev hesitantly, only to be met by groans from all corners of the room.

"Wear them tomorrow?" growled Lennie. "Against Hamley Hawks? Not likely! I mean – orange shirts! They'd think we were a right bunch of lemons!" Trev frowned. In daily life the Angels coach was the Reverend Trevor Rowe, vicar of St Jude's Church. All the Angels players were members of St Jude's Youth Club, and every year Trev led a shared weekend at the Leigh Country Park where they were joined by a group from another local youth club. This year it was to be the Hamley Hawks. The idea was that they all got to appreciate the countryside better by taking part in lots of different activities.

Everybody knew, though, that the highlight of the weekend was the Sunday afternoon football match between the two clubs. It was a game both teams were always desperate to win, because the tradition afterwards was for the losers to act as servants to the winners. In particular, this meant cleaning the huge dormitories they used. Even though they only slept in them on the Saturday night, it was still a job which could take hours!

Sighing, Trev held up the orange shirt again. "Correct me if I'm wrong, but do I get the impression that none of you are very keen on this football shirt?"

"It *is* bright," nodded Mick Ryall, taking off his glasses again to peer at the shirt. "There's that to say for it."

"Spot on, Mick," said Colly Flower. "Trev, it's terrible. It's too bright. The only thing worse would be finding it came with orange shorts and orange socks as well."

"It *does* come with orange shorts and orange socks as well," said Trev, glumly pulling a pair of each from his holdall.

"Not to mention…" He dipped into the holdall one more time and pulled out an altogether larger article, "a matching top for the coach!"

Lennie led the Angels into a huddle. Heads shook. Heads nodded. Finally, they separated with a loud cheer.

Trev brightened. "That's a bit more like it! Enthusiasm at last! You've made your decision, have you?"

"We have, Trev. We'll stick to our old white and blue strip – but you can keep your orange top!"

Having settled the shirts question, Trev
led the Angels out to the park's pitch for a
six-a-side game before the Hamley group
arrived. On the way he whispered in
Mick's ear. "Nobody in the team can
dribble like you, Mick. Nobody can send a
defender the wrong way like you! So, once
in a while I want you to go it alone. We'll
call it Plan 7D. Seven, for your shirt
number..."

"And D for 'Dribble'," said Mick.
"Right?"

"It's D for 'Dazzling', actually," smiled
Trev, "because that's what you'll need to be!"

It wasn't long before the coach decided
to test his plan. Seeing Mick receive the
ball on the right side of the pitch, Trev
yelled, "Plan 7D, Mick!"

Mick looked up. Ahead of him were
Ricky King, Rhoda O'Neill, Jeremy Emery

and – in goal – Kirsten Browne. As Mick
surged forward, Ricky came to meet him.
Hardly slowing, Mick feinted to go to his
left then, as Ricky moved that way,
suddenly darted to the right and sprinted
past him.

"Huh! You won't send *me* the wrong
way," muttered Rhoda O'Neill, turning
sideways on to force Mick to go outside
her.

"Oh no?" cried Mick. Pretending to cut inside, then outside, then inside again, he caused Rhoda to spin like a top and finally lose her balance altogether as he went by.

Next in line was Jeremy Emery, the Angels tall and gangly defender. Determined not to be fooled into going the wrong way, he decided not to go any way at all. Planted with his feet wide apart, he stood solidly in Mick's path – only to find the ball quickly slipped through his legs!

"A nutmeg!" laughed Mick, scuttling past. There was only Kirsten to beat, now.

Taking careful aim for the bottom corner of the net, he shaped to hit a screaming shot – only to stop his foot a centimetre from the ball. Like all the others, Kirsten was sent completely the wrong way. Soaring like an eagle towards one corner of her goal she could only watch helplessly as Mick calmly side-footed the ball into the other corner!

"Plan 7D a total success!" cried Mick, running back for the kick-off.

"Make the most of it, Four-Eyes," growled a voice from nearby. "'Cos your dribbling won't send me the wrong way!"

Unnoticed, the Hamley Hawks group had arrived and were watching from the touchline. The boy who'd spoken was in the middle of them. He had a haircut like a mown lawn that hadn't had the edges trimmed. The others round him were nodding in agreement.

"Says who?" smiled Mick, taking off his glasses and wiping away a couple of spots of rain.

"Says me," snapped the boy. "Bruiser Bloor's the name. And don't ask why they call me 'Bruiser'. You'll find out the first time I kick you."

Laughing, the Hamley group went to huddle under a tree to stay dry. Mick shrugged and went back to the game. But, with the rain getting heavier, he found himself having to wipe his glasses more and more often. Finally he took them off altogether and held them in his hand.

"Plan 7D!" called Trev, as the ball was played out to Mick once more.

Mick looked up. In front of him Ricky King, Rhoda O'Neill, Jeremy Emery and

Kirsten Browne were again barring his way.

Or were they? Without his glasses on, Mick really couldn't tell. Being very short-sighted, he could only see things really clearly if they were no more than a metre away. The trouble was, Ricky and the others *were* more than a metre away – which was why they all looked pretty blurry.

Undeterred, Mick zoomed off, dodging this way and that. Past Ricky King he went, then past Rhoda O'Neill – or so he thought until he heard Jonjo Rix shout, "What are you beating me for, Mick? I'm on your side!"

Squinting badly, Mick looked up. He

wanted to be aiming for the goal, and that meant Kirsten, with Jeremy Emery somewhere in front of her. He couldn't see Kirsten, but...

Yes, not too far away he could definitely see tall, thin Jeremy! By the look of him, the defender had taken a handkerchief out to blow his nose. Very helpful!

Keeping his eyes fixed on the handkerchief, Mick raced forward. Drawing close, he shimmied one way, ducked the other, then raced past. "Sent you the wrong way again, Jez!" yelled Mick – only to be brought to a halt by the screech of Trev's whistle.

"Goal kick to us," called Kirsten from somewhere away to his left.

"What? How?"

"Put your glasses back on and you'll see," giggled Kirsten.

Mick did so – and groaned. The fuzzy defender he'd just waltzed round hadn't been a thin, nose-blowing Jeremy at all. It had been a corner flag!

Looking on, all but one of the Hamley Hawks players had collapsed with laughter. The exception was Bruiser Bloor. He merely smiled a nasty smile.

"Well, look at that," he said to the others. "We ain't going to need to rough up tricky Micky at all. Without his glasses, he's useless. All we've got to do is pinch 'em..."

He grinned his toothy grin as another thought came to him. "Either that, or bust 'em..."

## 2

*Smash...or Grab*

By the time Mick Ryall and the other
Angels boys reached their dormitory after
the practice game, the Hamley Hawks
boys were already there. They'd taken
over the beds at one end of the dormitory
– and had already made a mess of it.

"Attention now!" called Trev. "Angels
and Hawks – I know it's tradition for the
losing team in the match on Sunday to
clear up the dormitory for the winners,
but that doesn't mean you shouldn't keep
it tidy until then."

From behind his back Trev produced a stiff-bristled broom in one hand, and a brush and pan in the other. The broom he gave to Lennie Gould, the brush and pan to Bazza Watts. "Show them how it's done, lads. Start sweeping!"

As Lennie and Bazza started work, the others dumped their things on the beds. Mick Ryall went for the bed in the corner nearest the door. Taking off his glasses, he placed them carefully on the blanket while he removed his damp football shirt.

Immediately, Bruiser Bloor appeared at his elbow. After what Bloor had been like earlier, Mick was expecting more threats. But, no, the Hawks player seemed to be a changed person.

"Hi! I didn't mean what I said about kicking you, y'know. That was just my little joke. I wouldn't hurt a fly. Not even a flying Angel! Ha ha!"

Bloor laughed. And laughed…

"Ha-ha! Ha-ha-ha! Ha-ha-ha-ha!" he roared, holding his middle and tottering backwards and forwards until he was almost on top of Mick's bed…

"Ha-ha-ha-ha-yeeeeoooooowwwwww!!" Bloor spun round, holding his backside.

Behind him, holding the stiff-bristled broom that had just jabbed him like a hundred needles, stood Lennie Gould.

"Sorry and all that," Lennie apologised, "but you were just about to squash Mick's glasses. By accident, of course."

Bruiser Bloor gave a weak smile. "Was I? Phew! Good job you stopped me."

"I think I'd better put them back on," said Mick.

"Allow me," said Bloor. He plucked Mick's glasses from the bed – only to let them slip from his fingers. "Oops!"

"You've dropped them!" yelled Mick.

"Howzat!" shouted a voice.

They all looked down. Bazza Watts, sweeping under the bed, had thrust out his arm to give Mick's glasses a soft landing in a dustpan full of fluff!

"You sure your nickname's Bruiser?" growled Lennie. "Butterfingers Bloor would be nearer the mark."

"Phew!" breathed Bloor again. "You could be right. That was another close shave! I'd put those glasses somewhere safe if I was you, Mick."

"Yeah," Bazza said to Bloor. "Somewhere miles away from you."

Mick slipped them on. "There. That's where they're safest. And I won't take them off until bedtime!"

Poking his head through the top of his Arsenal pyjamas, Mick yawned. They'd had a busy afternoon and evening and he was worn out. Removing and folding his glasses, he placed them carefully in his bedside cabinet.

"Mick!" hissed Lennie. "You can't leave them in there!"

"Why not?" said Mick.

"Because Bloor could swipe them while you're asleep," whispered Bazza, scuttling across from his own bed. He was quickly joined by the other Angels players. "We reckon he could come after them, see? He knows that without your glasses you're...er..."

"Useless," said Mick, remembering his dribble round the corner flag.

"Can't you sleep with them on?" asked Jeremy Emery.

"No! That way, *I'd* bust them!"

"I know!" cried Lionel Murgatroyd. "How about staying awake and watching over them?"

"Good one, Lionel!" said Mick. "Then I'll fall asleep in the middle of the game tomorrow, so I'll still be useless!"

Lionel shook his head. "I didn't mean *you*, Mick. I meant *us*. We all take it in turns to guard your glasses for an hour."

"Brilliant!" said Lennie. "I'll do the first hour. Then I'll wake up Jonjo to do the second hour, he can wake up Tarlock for the third hour, and so on."

They all turned to Mick and helped tuck him into bed.

"Dazzling dreams, Mick," cooed Colly. "Your specs are as safe as anything. Your guardian Angels are here to look after them!"

Sitting drowsily on the end of Mick's bed, Lionel glanced at his watch. By the pale light of the moon he saw that it said six minutes to four. Only another six minutes and he could wake up Ricky for his turn on guard duty.

Lionel's eyes began to droop. Quickly

he flicked them back open. He, of all
people, couldn't go to sleep on duty! It
had been his idea. A brilliant idea! They'd
all said so.

He looked at his watch again. Five
minutes to go. Maybe if he just stared at
the watch face it would help him
concentrate on staying awake.

Lionel focused hard. Four minutes to
go. It was working! Three
minutes to go. Two.
One. Only sixty
seconds to zero!

Zero, zero, zer…
zzzzzzzzzzzzzz…

3

*Keep Your Eyes Peeled!*

Mick was dreaming. He was desperately trying to set off on a mazy run through the Hamley Hawks defence. The trouble was, he couldn't move his feet. There seemed to be a heavy weight on top of them...

Blinking open his eyes, Mick sat up in bed – and discovered exactly why he'd been having that particular dream. It was because there *had* been a heavy weight on his feet. A fast-asleep Lionel Murgatroyd!

"Lionel!" hissed Mick, giving him a shake.

"Wha-wha-wassamarra?" gurgled Lionel, suddenly sitting bolt upright. "Four o'clock, is it? Time I was off duty?"

Mick snorted. "Four o'clock? It's eight o'clock, Lionel! It's Sunday morning and we're at the Country Park and the sun's shining and all's right with the world and you've obviously been snoring when you should have been guarding…and…and…"

"And what?" said Lionel, still rubbing the sleep from his eyes.

"And," wailed Mick, staring at the wide open door of his bedside cabinet, "my glasses have gone!"

Waiting until the Hawks went off to breakfast, the Angels searched the dormitory from top to bottom. Finding nothing, they then confronted Bruiser Bloor, surrounding him as he finished off a huge plate of bacon and eggs.

"Admit it, Bloor," snarled Rhoda O'Neill, "you pinched Mick's glasses during the night, didn't you?"

"Me?" laughed Bloor. "I haven't even *seen* his glasses!"

"A likely story," said Colly Flower.

"It's true!" Bloor put on an injured look. "Hey, I know what you're up to. You're trying to frame me, aren't you?"

He turned to the other Hawks with a grin. "Get it? *Frame* me! Glasses, frames…"

A cry from Trev interrupted the stream of bad jokes.

"Attention everybody! I expect you're already thinking about this afternoon's match, but forget man-to-man marking and all that for now. This morning it's our Treasure Hunt. Sort yourselves into groups of four or five, then get instruction sheets from me. Visit all the destinations and solve all the clues to win a prize!"

"Trev really likes that orange top, doesn't he?" sighed Mick, looking across to where Trev was standing at the far end of the room. "He's still wearing it."

"That's it!" hissed Lionel Murgatroyd suddenly. "That's how we might find out who's got your glasses! Trev's just given us the answer!"

"By wearing orange?" asked Jonjo.

"No," replied Lionel, "by man-to-man marking! If our groups forget all about the Treasure Hunt and just follow the Hawks groups everywhere, maybe one of us will spot something..."

"Nothing," groaned Lionel. "We've been following them for miles and they haven't given us a clue."

Lionel, Kirsten, Jonjo, Rhoda and Colly,

together with a squinting Mick himself, had been trailing Bruiser Bloor's group, trying to keep themselves out of sight while they watched what the Hawks were doing. They'd just stopped as, through the trees, Bruiser Bloor had halted his group and looked their way.

Moments later the Hawks captain boomed, "I think we're being *goggled at*, team! So – let's go!"

Caught by surprise, the Angels group gave chase as the Hawks disappeared along a narrow track. But with Mick needing to go fairly slowly to avoid running into things, the Hawks were soon out of sight – and, by the time the Angels reached a signpost at a junction with a number of other tracks, they were nowhere to be seen.

Something else was, though. From the signpost a hastily scrawled note was fluttering.

"This is a 'dazzling dribbling' signpost," read Colly. "What sort of clue is that?"

"A bad joke Bruiser Bloor clue, if you ask me," said Lionel. He began to pace up and down. "Now, let's think. Mick's a dazzling dribbler…"

"Only when I'm wearing my glasses," said Mick glumly.

"Right. So a 'dazzling dribbling'

signpost could be…one with a pair of glasses! I bet Bloor's just got rid of the evidence by hiding them round here somewhere!"

They all dropped to their knees and scrabbled in the long grass at the base of the signpost. Suddenly, Lionel gave a cry of triumph. "Got them!" he cried, holding up Mick's glasses.

Mick couldn't have been happier if he'd just found a long-lost brother. Kissing his glasses he rubbed them clean and put them on. But a worrying thought had struck Rhoda. She frowned.

"Why would Bloor leave a clue to help you find your glasses? That would be stupid."

Mick laughed as he gazed around. "Because Bloor *is* stupid! Now – which is the way back?"

They all looked up at the signpost. It clearly pointed them off along another, rather overgrown, track. With a spring in his step, Mick led the group down it. On they went, between trees and around brambles, as the track slowly got narrower and narrower…until finally it vanished altogether.

"Funny," said Kirsten. "That signpost definitely pointed this way."

Mick groaned. "Oh no! The note! I've just realised what a 'dazzling dribbling' signpost really is."

"What?" they all asked together.

"It's a signpost that sends you the wrong way! Bloor must have switched it round. That's why he didn't care about me finding my glasses again – because his plan was for us not to get back in time for the match. And it worked. We're lost!"

## 4

*No Smoke Without Fire*

"Now what do we do?" asked Kirsten.

"Wait here," said Jonjo. "Trev and the other Angels will come looking for us when we don't turn up."

"But what if they meet Bruiser Bloor?" said Lionel. "And he sends them the wrong way too?"

"They'll never find us!" wailed Rhoda. "We'll miss the match! The Angels will only have half a team! They'll win! We'll have to be their slaves!"

"Bad," said Mick.

Rhoda looked panic-stricken. "Bad? It's terrible! You want to see the state of the girls' dormitory! We turned that over looking for your glasses, too!"

"Then we need to do something to show them where we are," said Mick. He took off his glasses and polished them thoughtfully. "But what?"

"Shout!" squawked Rhoda, and immediately began hollering at the top of her voice. "Help! We're here! Yoo-hooooo!!!"

The others joined in, calling at the tops of their voices, until Jonjo said, "It's no good. They won't hear us unless they're close. What we need is something to attract their attention from miles away."

Mick snapped his fingers. "I've got it! A smoke signal! They'd be able to see that from miles away!"

"Er...small problem, Mick," said Jonjo. "No smoke without fire. And no fire without matches."

"Wrong, Jonjo," said Mick, noticing the shafts of strong sunlight cutting through the trees. "You lot gather something to burn. I know how to light the fire!"

Soon they'd collected a pile of dry twigs and wet leaves. Taking them to a clearing so that there was no danger of the fire accidentally spreading, they heaped the sticks together. That was when Mick bent down...and took off his glasses once more.

Holding them up to the sky, he moved them around until the rays of the sun, shining through one of the lenses, came together in a sharp, hot point of light on the twigs. Within seconds the twigs started to smoulder. Not long after, they began to smoke. And then, with a sudden little *whoosh*, they burst into flame!

Whooping delightedly, the others helped tip more wood on top until they had a good, crackling fire. Then on went the wet leaves – and out billowed thick smoke!

"And now, Squaw Rhoda, send signals to Big Chief Trev the Rev!"

Grabbing her rucksack, Rhoda held it over the bonfire so that some smoke became trapped underneath, then whipped it away to allow a big blob of smoke to sail upwards.

Soon a flock of smoky dollops was sailing high into the sky, visible for miles around. And not long after that, there came the distant sounds of shouting and footsteps ploughing through the undergrowth.

Mick swung round. "Here comes Trev!"

Beside him, Lionel blinked. "Trev? Where?"

"You need your eyes tested, Lionel," said Mick, pointing into the distance. "Can't you see his orange top?"

Lionel peered through the trees. "No."

Mick pointed again at the glow moving their way. "There!" He whipped his glasses off with a flourish. "Crikey, that top's so bright I can see it a mile away – and with only two eyes!" Slipping his glasses back on, Mick thumped his chest proudly. "We're saved, Lionel! Now brave Angels go fight afternoon battle with Hamley Hawks!" he cried. "And give them heap big whacking!"

## 5

## *A Red-Hot Display!*

Bruiser Bloor moved menacingly to Mick's side as the teams came out for the big challenge match later that afternoon.

"You're going to wish you'd stayed lost in the woods, Four-Eyes," he growled. "'Cos I'm going to give you bruises so big you'll be able to see 'em without your specs on!"

Bloor strode to his place in the Hamley Hawks defence, while Mick trotted out to his position on the right wing. Trev was standing on the touchline with Lionel

Murgatroyd and Ricky King, the Angels substitutes.

"Remember the Angels code, Mick," said Trev, who'd overheard Bruiser's threat. "'Angels on and off the field.' No dirty play. The referee will sort him out if he gets near you."

"He isn't going to get near me, Trev!" laughed Mick, adjusting his glasses and gazing around the pitch. "Not now I can see him coming!"

And, as the game got underway, Mick proved to be as good as his word. He was in sparkling form.

When Bloor came thundering in to tackle him, Mick simply slipped the ball inside to Colly Flower or another Angels player, skipped over the Hawks player's flailing boots, then ran off to collect the return pass.

After a few hopeless attempts, Bruiser stopped diving in and waited to see what Mick would do. When that happened Mick simply sent him the wrong way by dribbling up to him, feinting to go one way then darting the other before Bloor knew what had happened.

"Mick's playing brilliantly," said Trev to Lionel. "So...Plan 7D!" he hollered as the ball was pushed out to Mick yet again.

Hearing the call Mick set off at once, dribbling past one Hawks player after another. Approaching their penalty area, he was going at top speed.

Bruiser Bloor, finally realising what was happening, came racing in from the side and launched himself into a sliding tackle. But Mick had seen him coming. Stopping dead, his foot on the ball, he stood and watched as Bloor slithered in front of him like a snake in football gear. Only then did he set off again and clip the ball past the Hawks goalie and into the net.

1–0 to the Angels! Or was it?

Bruiser Bloor was still on the ground, holding his leg and yelling like mad. "Foul, ref! He trod on me! Send him off! I'm injured!"

"I didn't see anything," said the referee, puffing up.

"It was a foul, I tell you!" yelled Bloor. "He's broken my leg!"

With the referee starting to look more doubtful, Trev ran on to see what he could do to help. Behind him followed Lionel Murgatroyd holding the first-aid kit.

"I don't know what he's on about," hissed Mick to Lionel. "I didn't touch him!"

Trev bent down beside Bruiser. As he did so, the Hawks player let out an even louder cry of agony. "I'll never walk again! Just 'cos he wears glasses, it don't mean he's not dirty! Send him off, I say!"

"That's what he's on about!" said Lionel to Mick. "He's trying to get you sent off. He knows he can't cope with your dazzling dribbling…"

Even as he said the words, Lionel

looked up into the sky – and had an idea.
Quickly taking Mick's glasses from him,
he hurried over to give Trev the first-aid
kit. Then, bending down beside him, he
held Mick's glasses up to the sun until
the hot dot of light was just where he
wanted it…

"Yeeeooooooooooowwwwwwwwww!!!"
screamed Bruiser Bloor. Moments later
he'd leapt to his feet, knocking Lionel
flying as he did so, and was racing round
the penalty area holding his backside.

"It seems like he can walk after all,"
said the referee. "No foul! Goal allowed!"

"Looks like my glasses trick doesn't only set twigs on fire!" hooted Mick, hurrying across to Lionel. "Well done, Lionel!"

Lionel groaned. He seemed to be in pain.

"Are you all right?" said Mick. "You looked like you landed badly."

The Angels substitute lifted himself off the ground and pulled out something shapeless and mangled from beneath him.

He groaned again. "I did land badly. I landed on your glasses."

"That looks like the end of Plan 7D then, Mick," said Trev at half time. "Without your glasses you'll be beating players on our side as well as theirs."

Mick nodded glumly – until he suddenly realised that what Trev had said was wrong!

"No I won't, Trev," said Mick. "Because our players won't be trying to get the ball off me. The only players trying to tackle me will be Hawks, so I'll know they're the ones I have to beat!"

Feeling much happier, Mick scurried out for the start of the second half. He looked at the players around him. They were all very blurred and, unless he was quite close to them, even the Angels' white shirts didn't look too much different to the blue shirts worn by the Hamley Hawks. But that didn't matter. All he had to do was beat any player who came in to tackle him.

The chance came along fairly soon. Receiving a pass out on the touchline, Mick put his head down and raced towards the first blur.

"Come on then, Tricky Micky," growled the shape, "let's see you beat me."

It was Bruiser Bloor. Without slowing, Mick leaned to his left then dodged to his right. As he skipped past, though, the Hawks defender grabbed his arm and spun him round. Mick struggled free, the ball still at his feet. At once, Bloor seemed to give up. Mick's arm was released and he was away.

"No! Stop him!"

Hearing the shouts of alarm, Mick put a spurt on. Having escaped Bloor's clutches so easily, the Hawks obviously knew they were in trouble!

Side-stepping the first player who came towards him, he bamboozled the next and raced on. Now others were coming in to try to get the ball off him, desperate Hawks defenders complaining bitterly as he skipped round them.

Or were they Hawks defenders?

As he evaded another tackle, Mick thought he heard a voice, which sounded very much like that of Daisy Higgins, cry out, "I'm on your side!"

He dodged another tackle, this time to hear a voice sounding like Bazza Watts bellow, "Mick, you're going the wrong way!"

The wrong way? But how? Of course…
Bruiser Bloor! Spinning him round by the
arm had been deliberate. That's why he
hadn't given chase. He'd pointed him
towards his own goal!

Mick screeched to a halt – but the
damage had been done. Having taken the
ball through his own defence, all the
Hawks striker had to do was whip the ball
off Mick's toe and whack it past Kirsten in
the Angels goal to make the score 1–1!

Winning the ball back straight from the kick-off, Hamley Hawks swept forward, piling all their players into attack as they searched for the winner.

"Don't worry about him," yelled Bruiser Bloor to one of his defenders, who asked if he should stay back and mark Mick. "He won't be going anywhere."

To a miserable Lionel Murgatroyd, standing out on the touchline, it seemed as if Bloor was right. Mick was standing on his own on the half-way line, peering this way and that, as if he couldn't even work out which way to run if he did get the ball.

"It's all my fault," sighed Lionel. "It was me who busted his glasses."

"Don't blame yourself, Lionel," said Trev. "It's not your fault that Mick's short-sighted and can't see anything far off without glasses."

"He can see some things," replied Lionel. "Your orange shirt when you came looking for us, for instance. Mick didn't need his glasses on to see that."

"My orange—" began Trev.

He didn't finish. Instead, as a Hawks attack broke down and the ball was walloped upfield to relieve the pressure, he started sprinting.

"Plan 7D, Mick!" he yelled.

Out in the centre circle, Mick had the ball. With all the Hawks upfield he'd had the time he'd needed to bring it under control. He looked up. As ever, the grass and pitch markings nearby were in clear focus but everything looked blurry in the distance.

Even so, he could make out something. An orange blur, now coming to a halt somewhere far off.

And then he heard Trev's call. "Aim for the orange shirt!"

Mick set off, the ball at his feet, his eyes fixed on the orange target. On he ran until, suddenly, a goalkeeper-shaped blur emerged. A duck and a dodge and Mick was past him, still running, running, until another shape appeared – that of the Hawks goal and, standing right behind the net, Trev in his bright orange top!

All Mick had to do was run the ball between the posts!

2–1 to Angels!

From there on, Hamley Hawks couldn't leave Mick alone, and all the Angels had to do was play out time to win the match. As Bruiser Bloor and his team-mates skulked off to start cleaning the dormitories, the players crowded round to congratulate Mick.

"Thank Trev," said Mick. "I could see his orange top miles away!"

Lennie Gould stepped forward. "Then on behalf of the team, Trev, I'd like to say thank you very much for wearing that top..." Then, grinning at the others, he added, "...although it's still the most revolting colour in the world and none of us would be seen dead in it!"

"I suppose you're right," said Trev. "OK, forget the orange shirts. We stick to *angelic* white!"

"You've got to keep wearing that top though, Trev," said Mick amid the cheering.

"Why?" chorused the Angels.

"In case I smash my glasses again, of course. As far as I'm concerned that top of Trev's is a sight for sore eyes!"